# Lazy
# Daisy

In memory of *The Marques* and those who perished
when she sank near Bermuda in 1983.

1 3 5 7 9 10 8 6 4 2

Copyright © Rob Lewis 1994

Rob Lewis has asserted his right under the Copyright, Designs and Patents Act, 1988
to be identified as the author and illustrator of this work

First published in the United Kingdom 1994
by The Bodley Head Children's Books
Random House, 20 Vauxhall Bridge Road, London SW1V 2SA

Random House Australia (Pty) Limited
20 Alfred Street, Milsons Point, Sydney,
New South Wales 2061, Australia

Random House New Zealand Limited
18 Poland Road, Glenfield,
Auckland 10, New Zealand

Random House South Africa (Pty) Limited
PO Box 337, Bergvlei 2012, South Africa

Random House UK Limited Reg. No. 954009

A CIP catalogue record for this book is available from the British Library

ISBN 0 370 31806 4

Printed in China

# Lazy
# Daisy

BY
ROB LEWIS

The Bodley Head
London

Daisy was a sea cat.
She lived on a trading ship
that carried grain and
spices from faraway
places across the oceans.

All day she dozed
amongst the ropes in
the hot sun.
'That cat is lazy!' growled
the captain. 'All she does is
eat and sleep.'
Daisy opened one eye, yawned,
stretched and went back to sleep.

'There are rat holes in the sails,' grumbled the sailmaker.
'There are dirty rat footprints on the charts,' moaned the first mate.
'There are rat teeth marks in the salt beef,' complained the purser.
'Where's that useless cat?' roared the captain. 'I'll throw it overboard!'
'Don't do that, captain,' pleaded the cook's boy, who liked cats.
'Very well,' mumbled the captain, 'but unless that cat starts catching rats soon, I will sell her at the next port!'

Daisy had been sitting on
the yardarm, listening.
She didn't want to be a land cat.
She loved the sea life.
She would have to catch some rats.

Down in the hold, she prowled amongst the sacks trying to look
fierce. Perhaps the rats would be frightened away. The rats sat
on top of a pile of barrels, laughing.
'Stupid, lazy cat,' they said.

One rat nibbled a hole in a sack.
Out poured a stream of flour on to Daisy's head.

'Useless cat!' scowled the purser, when he saw Daisy.

The cook's boy gave Daisy some cheese.
'See if you can catch some rats with this,' he said.
Daisy climbed into a coil of rope and waited for a rat
to come and nibble at the cheese.

'Stupid, lazy cat,'
laughed the rats.
They scurried up the
mast and gnawed through
the ropes that held one of
the sails. Down it came on
top of Daisy.

'Asleep again?' sighed the sailmaker, when he found Daisy.

Daisy crept down to the
very bottom of the ship
and sniffed for rat holes
amongst the brandy casks.

'Stupid, lazy cat,' said the rats. They pulled the bungs out of some casks. 'Drunken cat!' hissed the first mate, when he found Daisy in a pool of brandy.

'The rats on this ship are worse than ever!'
said the captain. 'Tomorrow in port
I shall sell that cat!'

Poor Daisy. She had never caught a rat before and these were very clever rats.

That night there was a terrible storm.
Wind battered the sails and
waves crashed over the decks.

The first mate was at the wheel.
Suddenly he was washed across the deck.

The captain came to help
the first mate.
'We must steer the ship away
from the rocks,' said the captain.
Together they struggled to get
to the wheel against the wind
and waves.
'We shall all be drowned!'
wailed the first mate.

Then, through the rain, they saw the wheel.
'Look at that!' said the captain.
'I don't believe it!' said the first mate.
There was Daisy holding the wheel steady with her paws.
She had saved the ship from hitting the rocks.

'Clever cat,' said the sailmaker, the next morning.
'Brave cat!' said the purser.
'Well done, Daisy,' said the cook's boy.
'I certainly won't sell you,' said the captain, and
he placed his cap on Daisy's head.
She felt very proud.
And what happened to the rats?
During the storm - like all cowardly rats...

...they left the sinking ship!